D1266152

SCOOBY-DOO!

THE ALIENS OF AREA 49

by **SCOTT GROSS** with
DAVID RODRIGUEZ--colorist
TRAVIS LANHAM--letterer
CHYNNA CLUGSTON
FLORES--asst. editor
SCOTT PETERSON--editor

Spotlight

visit us at www.abdopublishing.com

Reinforced library bound edition published in 2013 by Spotlight, a division of the ABDO Group, PO Box 398166, Minneapolis, MN 55439. Spotlight produces high-quality reinforced library bound editions for schools and libraries. Published by agreement with Warner Bros.-A Time Warner Company.

Printed in the United States of America, North Mankato, Minnesota.
102012
082013
♻This book contains at least 10% recycled materials.

Library of Congress Cataloging-in-Publication Data

Gross, Scott.
 Scooby-Doo and the aliens of Area 49 / writer, Scott Gross ; penciller, David Rodriguez. -- Reinforced library bound edition.
    pages cm. -- (Scooby-Doo graphic novels)
 ISBN 978-1-61479-049-5
 1. Graphic novels. I. Scooby-Doo (Television program) II. Title. III. Title: Aliens of Area 49.
 PZ7.7.G78Sc 2013
 741.5'973--dc23

                    2012033322

All Spotlight books are reinforced library bindings and manufactured in the United States of America.

SCOOBY-DOO!

Table of Contents

THE ALIENS OF AREA 49 4

The Ghost of Christmas Presents 14

THE ALIENS OF AREA 49

by SCOTT GROSS with
DAVID RODRIGUEZ–colorist
TRAVIS LANHAM–letterer
CHYNNA CLUGSTON
FLORES–asst. editor
SCOTT PETERSON–editor

READY FOR *HOLIDAY SHOPPING,* GANG?

IT'S SO HARD TO SHOP FOR MY FATHER. HOW DO YOU GET SOMETHING FOR THE MAN WHO HAS EVERYTHING?

LIKE, *I* KNOW, DAPHNE--

-- THE NEW *"MIGHTY MITE BYTES II"* VIDEO GAME!

THAT'S WHAT A *REAL* FRIEND WOULD GET THEIR PAL -- I MEAN, *DAD!* RIGHT, SCOOB?

REAH, REAH! RIGHTY RITES!

LIKE, A *SWEATER,* VELMA? WOULDN'T *"THEY"* RATHER GET *MIGHTY MITE BYTES II?*

RUH-HUH!

HEY, *"THE WORLD'S GREATEST UNSOLVED MYSTERIES"!*

LOOK! *"TIPS ON MIGHTY MITE BYTES II!"*

GEE, IF ONLY I HAD THAT GAME...

SAY, SCOOB, HAVE YOU HEARD OF THE NEW *MIGHTY MITE BYTES* GAME? THAT'S SPELLED M-I-G--

SHAGGY, WE *KNOW!* WE *KNOW!*

LIKE, I'M JUST TRYING TO HELP!

TAKE IT EASY, GUYS! HERE, MAYBE SOME SCOOBY SNACKS WILL LIFT YOUR HOLIDAY SPIRITS!

BURGER MAX

SCOOBY SNACKS

ROOBY RACKS! ROBOY OBOY OBOY!

I KNOW SHAGGY WANTS IT--

--BUT IT'S *IMPOSSIBLE* TO FIND THAT GAME!

MUNCH MUNCH

WE'VE LOOKED *EVERY-WHERE!*

I CALLED EVERY STORE, CHECKED THE NET, EVEN LOOKED FOR A BOOTLEG COPY! NO ONE HAS ONE!

IT'S STRANGE, GANG! ALMOST A--

--MYSTERY!

LIKE, LOOK, SCOOB!

RASP!

HUH?!

MIGHTY MITE BYTES II! THE *PERFECT* GIFT FOR THE SPECIAL SOMEONE!

RIDEO RAMES! RAY!

MIGHTY MITE BYTES II

The Ghost of Christmas Presents

writer: JOHN ROZUM
artist: TIM HARKINS
letters: JOHN COSTANZA
colors: PAUL BECTON
ghosts: DANA KURTIN & CHUCK KIM

RUN, SCOOB!

SKID SKID

BONK

BLUE FALCON

THANKS, BLUE FALCON! I OWE YOU ONE!

YIKES!

SKREE! SKREE!

RUN FOR YOUR LIVES!

OH NO-- I KNEW I SHOULDN'T HAVE MENTIONED THE M-WORD!

WELL, AT LEAST THERE'S NO LINE ANY-MORE.

LIKE, I WANTED TO PLAY MIGHTY MITE BYTES II-- BUT NOT AS THE BYTE!

WAIT, COME BACK! IF YOU DON'T BUY THIS GAME, I'LL GO OUT OF BUSINESS!

WHAT A STRANGE PROMOTIONAL GIMMICK! USUALLY YOU WANT TO ATTRACT CUSTOMERS--

--NOT SCARE THEM AWAY!

MIGHTY MITE BYTES

IT'S NO GIMMICK!

NO ONE IS SELLING THE GAME--BECAUSE OF THAT GHOST!

GHOST?!

RHOST?!

IT WOULDN'T LET THE DRIVERS EVEN LEAVE THE GAME FACTORY!

ONLY ONE TRUCK GOT THROUGH--TO MY STORE! BUT THE GHOST CAME WITH IT!

LIKE, OH NO! I HADDA WANT A HAUNTED CHRISTMAS PRESENT!

COME ON, SHAGGY!

LET'S SOLVE THIS MYSTERY! WILL YOU DO IT FOR-- A SCOOBY SNACK?

SCOOBY

ALL RIGHT, YOU TALKED ME INTO IT. LET'S GO, SCOOB!

REAH! SLURRRP!

SHAGGY, HOW DO YOU *STOP* THIS THING?

WELL, BY SPITTING *FIRE* OR GROWING *PLANTS* OR--

--OPENING DOORS.

WHUDD!

MOAN... MY HEAD!

DOES THE GHOST *DO* THAT IN THE GAME?

NO, BECAUSE THIS *ISN'T* A GHOST!

RIGHT! IT'S THE MAN WHO CREATED *MIGHTY MITE BYTES!*

THE RED FELT I FOUND *HAD* TO COME FROM A COSTUME.

AND ONLY SOMEONE WHO KNEW WHAT THE TOP-SECRET VILLAIN *LOOKED* LIKE COULD MAKE A COSTUME OF HIM!

PLUS IT HAD TO BE SOMEONE WHO HAD A PERSONAL STAKE IN STOPPING THE GAME FROM SHIPPING--

--AND THIS MAGAZINE IN THE STOREROOM SAID THE PROGRAMMER *SPLIT* WITH THE COMPANY OVER THE GAME!

BYTES CREATOR BITES DUST

THAT'S RIGHT! THEY WERE SHIPPING THE GAME FOR CHRISTMAS EVEN THOUGH IT HAD BIG PROBLEMS!

THE GAME'S NO GOOD?

LIKE, OH NO!

I DIDN'T MEAN ANY HARM-- I JUST DIDN'T WANT ALL THOSE KIDS TO GET ROTTEN GAMES.

WELL...IT *IS* THE HOLIDAYS, AND NO ONE GOT HURT. BUT NEXT TIME, WORK OUT YOUR PROBLEMS FACE TO FACE-- NOT AS A *GHOST!*

WELL, WHAT ARE WE GOING TO GIVE SHAGGY FOR CHRISTMAS NOW?

TELL YOU WHAT!

HERE'S THE PROTOTYPE OF MY NEWEST GAME--

-- YOU CAN TEST PLAY IT FOR ME.

MIGHTY MITE BYTES II

OH BOY!

THIS IS THE BEST PRESENT EVER!

I'M ALWAYS LOOKING FOR IDEAS FOR NEW GAMES!

FOUR MYSTERY-SOLVING KIDS AND A DOG...

...HMMN! HAS POTENTIAL!

ZOINKS! HIGH SCORE!

ROOBY ROOBY ROO!

HA HA HA!!

THE END